Being Friends

by Karen Beaumont
pictures by Joy Allen

Dial Books for Young Readers

NEW YORK

Published by Dial Books for Young Readers
A division of Penguin Young Readers Group
345 Hudson Street
New York, New York 10014
Text copyright © 2002 by Karen Beaumont
Pictures copyright © 2002 by Joy Allen
Designed by Nancy R. Leo-Kelly
Text set in OptiPowell Oldstyle
Manufactured in China on acid-free paper
17 18 19 20

Library of Congress Cataloging-in-Publication Data
Beaumont, Karen.
Being friends / by Karen Beaumont ; pictures by Joy Allen.
p.   cm.
Summary: Two very different girls find that the joy of being friends
enables them to share their various likes and dislikes.
ISBN 978-0-8037-2529-4
[1. Friendship—Fiction. 2. Individuality—Fiction. 3. Stories in rhyme.]
I. Allen, Joy, ill. II. Title.
PZ8.3.B3845 Be 2002   [E]—dc21   00-035865

For Kate and Carol, my delightfully
abnormal writer-friends, without whom this book
would not have come into being.

K.B.

To Rachel,
a wonderful friend and granddaughter!
And to my lifelong friends—
Ron & Mariel, Anita and Marilynn.

J.A.

I am me
and you are you.
I like red
and you like blue.

I like purple. You do too!
We both like being friends.

You are you
and I am me.
You're a princess sipping tea.

I'm a swinging chimpanzee.

You like makeup,
gems, and jewels.

I like spaceships,
rocks, and tools.
We both like being friends.

I like jeans
and you like gowns.
I like caps
and you like crowns.

I like hanging upside down.
You like twirling round
and round.

I do cartwheels.
You jump rope.

We both look through the telescope.
We both like being friends.

You like cookies.
I like cake.
Which will we decide to bake?

Eeny, meeny, miny, mo!
Sift the flour!
Stir the dough!

I like adding 2 plus 3.
You like spelling C-A-T.

I like books you read to me.
We both like being friends.

I'm a monster.
You're a queen.
We trick-or-treat on Halloween.

We both like spooky stories. . . .
BOO!

You hate mushrooms.
I hate peas.

Pepperoni pizza,
PLEASE!

I like jumping on the bed.
You like standing
on your head.

I like mornings.
You like nights.
We both like having pillow fights.
We both like being friends.

I like Saturn.
You like Mars.
We both like counting falling stars.

I pretend that I am you.
Copycat!
You do it too!

Sometimes we may play all day.
Sometimes we need time away.

I like you
and you like me,
and though we're different as can be...

we both like being friends!